Orange
Pear
Apple
Bear

For Mik

First
published
in 2006 by
Macmillan Children's
Books, a division of
Macmillan Publishers Limited
20 New Wharf Road, London
N1 9RR, Basingstoke and Oxford
Associated companies throughout
the world. www.panmacmillan.com
ISBN 1 405 05080 2
A CIP catalogue record for this
book is available from the British
Library. Printed in China.
1 3 5 7 9 8 6 4 2

Orange
Pear
Apple
Bear

Emily Gravett

Macmillan Children's Books

Orange

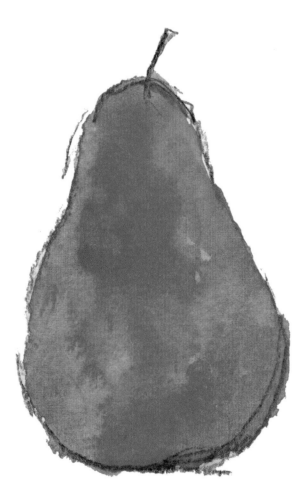

Pear

Apple

Bear

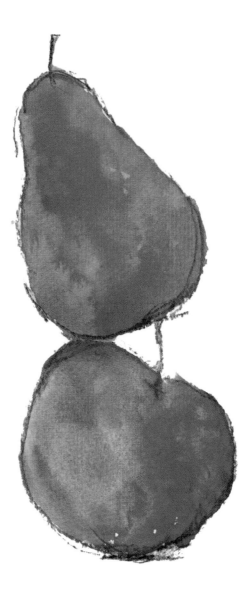

Apple, pear

Orange bear

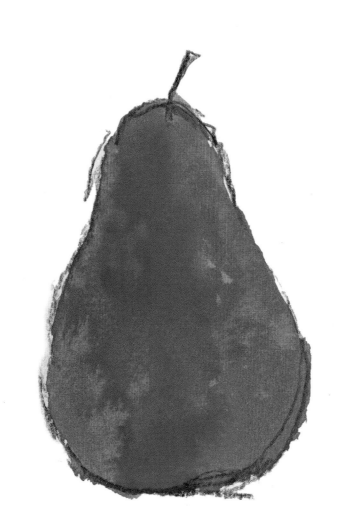

Orange pear

Apple bear

Apple, orange, pear bear

Orange, pear, apple, bear

Apple,

bear,

orange,

pear

Orange, bear

Pear, bear

There!

There!

Apple, bear